Magic
Animal
Rescue

Maggie and the Flying Pigs

Also by E. D. Baker

The Tales of the Frog Princess:
*The Frog Princess, Dragon's Breath,
Once Upon a Curse, No Place for Magic,
The Salamander Spell, The Dragon Princess,
Dragon Kiss, A Prince among Frogs,
The Frog Princess Returns*

*Fairy Wings
Fairy Lies*

Tales of the Wide-Awake Princess:
*The Wide-Awake Princess, Unlocking the Spell,
The Bravest Princess, Princess in Disguise,
Princess between Worlds, The Princess and the Pearl*

A Question of Magic

The Fairy-Tale Matchmaker:
*The Fairy-Tale Matchmaker,
The Perfect Match, The Truest Heart,
The Magical Match*

Magic Animal Rescue:
*Maggie and the Flying Horse,
Maggie and the Wish Fish, Maggie and the Unicorn*

Magic
Animal
Rescue

Maggie and the Flying Pigs

E. D. Baker

illustrated by
Lisa Manuzak

BLOOMSBURY

NEW YORK   LONDON   OXFORD   NEW DELHI   SYDNEY

First published in the United States of America in October 2017
by Bloomsbury Children's Books
www.bloomsbury.com

Bloomsbury is a registered trademark of Bloomsbury Publishing Plc

For information about permission to reproduce selections from this book,
write to Permissions, Bloomsbury Children's Books,
1385 Broadway, New York, New York 10018
Bloomsbury books may be purchased for business or promotional use. For
information on bulk purchases please contact Macmillan Corporate and
Premium Sales Department at specialmarkets@macmillan.com

Library of Congress Cataloging-in-Publication Data
available upon request
ISBN 978-1-68119-485-1 (paperback) • ISBN 978-1-68119-489-9 (hardcover)
• ISBN 978-1-68119-490-5 (e-book)

Book design by Jeanette Levy and Colleen Andrews
Typeset by Westchester Publishing Services
Printed and bound in the U.S.A.
by Berryville Graphics Inc., Berryville, Virginia
2 4 6 8 10 9 7 5 3 1 (paperback)
2 4 6 8 10 9 7 5 3 1 (hardcover)

All papers used by Bloomsbury Publishing, Inc., are natural, recyclable
products made from wood grown in well-managed forests. The
manufacturing processes conform to the environmental regulations of the
country of origin.

*This book is dedicated to daydreamers
and kids with "overactive" imaginations.
Let your imagination loose and you
can go far!*

Magic
Animal
Rescue

Maggie and the Flying Pigs

Chapter 1

Maggie laughed when one piglet tripped over another and they both tumbled across the floor. Although Maggie always enjoyed helping out in Bob's stable, she especially loved taking care of the flying pig and her babies. Still chuckling, Maggie dumped the bucket of grain into the mother pig's feed pan.

"What's so funny?" Leonard, the talking horse, asked from the next stall.

"The piglets are so cute!" Maggie told him. "I love the little sounds they make."

"Hunh!" he grunted. "That's one thing I could do without. Those 'cute' little sounds keep me awake half the night."

Maggie no longer thought it was unusual to have a conversation

with a talking horse, but then, she was used to a lot of unusual things happening at the stable where her friend Bob the Stableman took care of rare and magical creatures. Maggie had been helping Bob with the stable chores for a few weeks now. Bob and his wife, Nora, had taken Maggie in when her stepmother, Zelia, had kicked her out of the family cottage. Maggie loved her new family and thought it was a big improvement over her stepmother and stepsiblings. She missed her father every day, though. She wondered what he would do when he came home from chopping wood on the other side of the Enchanted Forest and found that his daughter was gone.

The mother pig lurched to her feet and ambled to her feed pan. Maggie hurried out of the way. The pig's wings looked a little tattered. Her babies must have been chewing on them again.

After stepping out of the stall and latching the door behind her, Maggie sat down on a bale of hay. Reaching into her pocket, she took out the brand-new journal that Bob had given her and opened it to one of the pages she'd started. She read over what she'd already noted.

Flying pigs:

Temperament—A mother flying pig can be very grumpy. Stay out of her way! Never get between the mother pig and her babies or her food.

Piglets—Baby flying piglets are very cute! They start running around fifteen minutes after they are born. At first their wings are just little stubs covered in fuzz.

Maggie took out her pencil and started to add to the page:

Once they get teeth, flying piglets like to chew on their mother's wings.
If she doesn't tuck her wings out of the way, her babies can chew holes in them. Sometimes the piglets tug so hard that the mother nips at them. Do not try to stop them or she might nip you!

Chapter 2

Maggie knew she shouldn't touch the piglets when their mother, Carmelita, was watching, but one baby was lying on its back, wedged in the corner of the stall, kicking the air with its little trotters. The piglet looked as if it was stuck. She couldn't just leave it there!

Moving slowly so she didn't startle the pigs, Maggie walked around the edge of the stall and reached for the baby. When Carmelita snorted and lurched to her feet, Maggie turned the baby so it could get up, then started running to the stall door. She could hear the mother pig charging after her.

With only

seconds to spare, Maggie threw herself at the half door, grabbing the top with both hands. Heaving herself up and over, Maggie felt the sow's teeth graze her shoe. The door shook as the mother pig crashed into it.

"What are you doing?" Leonard asked. He was a regular horse, except for the fact that he could talk. "It sounds as if you're trying to knock down the stable!"

"I was just helping a piglet," Maggie said, inspecting her shoe.

"If you made Carmelita mad, I suggest you shut the top door, too," said Leonard. "She is a flying pig, remember?"

Maggie gasped and turned around. She hadn't seen the sow fly lately and had forgotten that she *could* fly. Maggie heard the whoosh of beating wings and slammed the top half of the door shut. She had scarcely latched it when the sow crashed into it again. The angry squeals were loud enough to make Maggie cover her ears.

"Keep in mind that there are no ordinary animals here," Leonard reminded her.

"Says the talking horse," Maggie said with a laugh.

Leonard snorted and peered over his stall door. "I must say, you've been busy today. I don't think I've ever seen this barn look so clean."

Maggie shrugged. "I didn't do that much. I just cleaned the stalls like I usually do, and washed the water buckets."

"And swept out all the nooks

and crannies, and knocked down spider webs, and brushed me and Randal," Leonard reminded her. "Thanks for that, by the way. I know I feel a lot better, and Randal does too. The old unicorn has never looked so good. He really likes that you polished his horn."

"I'm glad," Maggie said.

Randal was the only unicorn who had a permanent home in the stable. Years before, Bob had found him caught in a trap with his leg horribly mangled. Bob had brought him home, but the unicorn's leg was so badly injured that it had to be replaced with a peg leg made out of wood. The unicorn loved Maggie, who always went out of her way to make him more comfortable.

"The sheriff stopped by," Bob said as he walked into the stable. "I was just telling him what a hard worker you are, Maggie."

Maggie's stepmother, Zelia, had kicked Maggie out of the family cottage a few weeks before. Ever

since then, Maggie had lived with
Bob and his wife, Nora. She loved
the elderly couple as much as if they
were her own family and was

always happy to help out. Still, three things worried her even from her safe new home: When would her father return from cutting wood on the far side of the Enchanted Forest? What would happen with her stepmother when he did? And what would her obnoxious stepbrother Peter do next?

Carmelita squealed and banged into her door so hard that the entire wall shook.

"What's wrong with her?" asked Bob.

"Maggie helped one of her piglets," explained Leonard.

Maggie nodded. "The baby was stuck and couldn't get up."

"Carmelita is mad because she wasn't able to take a chunk out of Maggie," Leonard finished.

"I'm not surprised," said Bob. "The sow's been going a little stir-crazy lately. I think I should take her outside and let her stretch her wings."

"Aren't you afraid she might fly off?" Maggie asked.

"Not with her babies here. I've tended mother flying pigs before. She'll come back in a few hours and be in a much better mood. Stay out of sight while I take her outside, Maggie. She's mad at you now, but she won't be by the time she gets back."

"You can brush me some more," Leonard told Maggie. "There's an itchy spot on my back that really needs it!"

Maggie groaned, but smiled and looked for the brush.

Chapter 3

Maggie was collecting Leonard's brush and currycomb when she heard squealing and the rustling of straw in the pigs' stall. She opened the top door just a crack so she could see inside. Most of the piglets were scurrying around, crying for their mother and beating their little wings that had grown feathers only a few days before. Maggie couldn't help but smile when she saw some take tiny hops and rise a few inches into the air.

"How are the babies doing?" Bob asked as he joined her at the stall door.

"I think they're getting ready to fly," said Maggie.

Bob smiled. "Perfect! We can give them their first lesson while their mother is outside."

"Shouldn't their mother teach them?" Maggie asked.

"She'll try, but I've found that it's better for the piglets if they know how to fly before her lessons start," said Bob. "Mother flying pigs are very rough when they teach their babies. They chase them, nipping at their heels until the babies take off. Sometimes they step on the ones that can't fly yet.

Piglets that are slow at learning to fly often get badly injured. I try to give them a head start, if I can. Stay here. I'll be right back. I have to get the blanket."

"Why do you need a blanket?" Maggie asked.

"You'll see," Bob called as he left the stable.

Maggie was still waiting for Bob when her friend Stella and Stella's goose, Eglantine, walked in. After shutting the goose in an empty stall, Stella joined Maggie.

"Where's Carmelita?" Stella asked, looking into the pigs' stall.

"Outside stretching her wings," Maggie told her.

"Oh, good!" Bob said when he saw Stella. "We could give the lesson with two people, but it will work even better with three. Here, you two hold the blanket and I'll toss the piglets. The babies that can fly will take off. You'll hold the blanket to catch the ones that can't."

"Is this safe?" asked Stella.

"I haven't lost a piglet yet!" Bob replied. "You girls stand over there and use both hands to hold the blanket. That's it! Now wait until I catch a piglet. All right. Here goes!"

Maggie and Stella braced their legs while Bob tossed a piglet at the blanket. Maggie expected to have to catch it, but to her surprise the little pig started beating its wings as soon as Bob let it go. It flew off, landing halfway across the stall.

"That was amazing!" Stella cried as Maggie laughed in delight.

"Get ready! Here comes the next one," warned Bob.

The next baby pig flew as well, making it all the way across the stall. A few of the piglets were able to make a circuit around the girls. Only two didn't flap their wings and landed in the blanket.

"That was so much fun!" exclaimed Stella. "Can we do it again tomorrow?"

"If the weather is good and I'm able to let Carmelita out," said Bob. "Once all the babies can fly, it won't be long before we release mother and babies into the forest."

"Speaking of releasing animals into the forest," said Leonard, "I'd love to take someone for a ride."

"I need to get home," said Stella. "My mother is baking a cake for my little brother's birthday and I promised I'd help."

"And Nora wants me to fix the

front door. The latch isn't working properly," Bob told them.

"Then I guess I'm your volunteer," Maggie told Leonard. "It should be fun! It's a beautiful day out."

"And I know just where I want to go," the horse told her. "I haven't visited the waterfall in a very long time."

Chapter 4

Although Maggie hadn't had much experience with horses before she came to live with Bob and Nora, she'd ridden Leonard a number of times by now. Both Maggie and Leonard enjoyed their outings together, so she was looking forward to riding him to the waterfall. The journey wasn't long, and it took them only a few minutes to reach the falls.

Leonard nickered when he saw the splashing water and trotted to the pool beneath the falls without any direction from Maggie. The horse was drinking when Maggie slid off his back. A head popped out of the water a moment later, and her friend Lily,

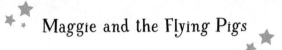

the water nymph, waved to her.
"How are you today?" called Lily.

"Great!" Maggie called back, walking to the edge of the pool. "Leonard offered to take me for a ride and wanted to come here."

The horse raised his head and water dribbled from his lips. "The water in your pool is delicious," he said. "Very clean and fresh."

"Have I ever told you that Leonard is a talking horse?" Maggie asked Lily.

"How fascinating!" cried Lily. "I didn't know that such creatures existed."

"Huh," said Leonard. "A lot of people don't believe that water nymphs exist. I think a talking horse makes a lot more sense than a girl who lives with fish."

Noticing the annoyed look on Lily's face, Maggie tried to change the subject. "Have you seen the palomino unicorn lately? When we let him go near here, I thought he might stay around."

"He did!" said Lily. "I see him every day. He's gotten to be very friendly. Yesterday he came right up to me and let me scratch his neck."

"Well, look what we have here!" someone said from deeper in the forest.

As soon as Lily heard the voice, she sank into the water and peeked out from among the waterlilies.

Maggie knew that voice. It was her stepbrother Peter. When she finally spotted him, he was carrying a long stick and whacking the underbrush as he walked.

"Hello, Peter," Maggie said.

"Couldn't you be a little more enthusiastic?" asked Peter. "After all, I am your brother."

"Stepbrother," said Maggie. "Why do you keep coming here? You're awfully far from home."

"I came to see you, dear sister. Mother wants to know that you're all right."

"That's hard to believe," said Maggie. "She's the one who kicked me out of my own cottage."

"You only got what you deserved," Peter began. "You're a worthless . . ."

"It's time to go," Leonard told Maggie. "There's something about this place that I find really annoying."

The horse walked to Maggie and bent down, making it easy for her to climb on his back. They were passing Peter when the boy whacked Leonard hard with his stick.

Leonard wheeled around and his

back feet shot out, kicking Peter into the pool. The boy landed in the water with a huge splash. He spluttered and stood up, looking furious.

"I know you don't know much about horses, Peter, so here's an important tip," said Maggie. "Never hit a horse with a stick like that. They don't like it one bit."

Leonard nickered with laughter when he saw the expression on Peter's face. This only seemed to make Peter madder as he waded out of the water and stomped away.

"That's one way to make him leave," said Lily.

"It definitely worked," said Maggie. "But I really do want to know what he was doing here."

Chapter 5

That afternoon, Maggie sat under a tree near the stable to work on her journal. Turning to a fresh page in the section about flying pigs, she wrote:

Teaching flying piglets to fly:

Mother flying pigs can be very mean. They nip at their babies and chase them to make them fly. It is better to teach the babies to fly while the mother is outside stretching her wings. You need 2 or 3 people for the lesson. One person throws the piglets. The others use a blanket to catch the piglets that can't fly yet.

After stretching her wings, the mother pig is much happier and a lot less grumpy. She is also very tired. When she rejoins her babies, she lies down and takes a long nap. The babies are happier, too. Their mother is sound asleep and doesn't nip at them if they get rough when they play.

When she was finished writing, Maggie drew some pictures of the piglets and their mother. She was sitting back, rereading what she'd just written, when she heard a small child crying. Maggie set down the journal and her pencil as she stood up and looked around. The crying sounded as if it was coming from the woods.

"Help me!" wailed a child's voice. Maggie thought it sounded like Maeve, one of her youngest step-sisters.

Maggie ran into the forest. "Maeve, is that you?" she called. "I'm coming!"

"I'm over here!" the child cried from deeper in the forest.

Maggie hurried as fast as she could. She climbed over fallen logs and ducked under low branches. "Where are you now?" she called. There was no answer. "Is anyone there?"

A twig snapped somewhere in the forest. A big owl hooted.

No one responded to Maggie's call.

Worried, Maggie looked everywhere. She searched behind trees, but some nasty squirrels threw nuts at her. She peered into prickly bushes that scratched her arms and face. Getting down on her hands and knees, she looked in a small cave where a snake raised its head and hissed. Finally, Maggie gave up and went back to the tree where she'd left her journal. Her pencil was there, but her journal was gone.

Maggie was sure she'd left it beside the tree. She knew she hadn't taken it into the woods! Looking carefully, Maggie searched all around the tree, even under the arching roots. The journal wasn't there, either.

"Maybe a raccoon carried it into the tree," she said, peering at the branches. Grabbing hold of the lowest branch, she pulled herself up and started to look. She inspected every branch and twig, startling a finch in her nest. When she peeked into a big hole in the trunk, two baby owls blinked at her from the depths. She even climbed to the top of the tree and surveyed the ground nearby. The journal wasn't anywhere in sight.

Maggie was more upset than

ever when she scrambled out of the tree. Her journal was definitely gone! Unable to figure out what had happened, she went to the cottage to see Bob. He was sitting at the kitchen table with Nora. They both looked up when Maggie walked in.

"My journal is gone," she told them, close to tears. "I've looked everywhere!"

"Where did you have it last?" asked Nora.

"I was sitting under the old oak

writing about the piglets when I heard a child crying in the woods. I went to see if I could help, but there wasn't anyone there. When I went back to get my journal, it was gone. I *know* I left it at the bottom of the tree!"

"A crying child, you say?" said Bob. "The only small children who live around here are in the castle, and they don't come out to play in the forest by themselves. Did it sound like anyone you know?"

Maggie nodded. "I thought it sounded like my little stepsister, Maeve."

"I see," said Bob. "I know it's upsetting to lose something you treasure, but in this case I'm sure it will show up in a few days. If it doesn't, I have a good idea where to start looking."

"Do you think Peter took it?" Maggie asked.

Bob nodded. "I wouldn't be surprised."

Chapter 6

Maggie gave the unicorn's horn one last swipe with the polishing rag and stepped back to admire her handiwork. The horn glistened in the sunlight pouring through the stall window. Pale blue and silver, it looked beautiful against the unicorn's white coat.

Randal snorted and shook his head, tossing the mane Maggie had just brushed. His coat glistened from being brushed, too, but she knew that wouldn't last long. He would roll and get dirty again as soon as she let him out in one of the paddocks. Having one wooden leg didn't stop Randal from having fun.

"That beast has only three legs!" Peter said from the doorway. "Why do you keep it around?"

"What are you doing here, Peter?" Maggie asked.

"I came to see Bob," he said, smirking.

"Bob!" Maggie called without taking her eyes off her step-brother. "Peter wants to talk to you."

Bob came out of the end stall where he'd been fixing a broken board. When he saw Peter, he nodded as if he'd been expecting him.

"I found something that I think belongs to you," Peter said, opening a cloth bag. He pulled out Maggie's journal and handed it to Bob. Glancing at Maggie, Peter's smirk grew broader.

"Maggie left your book in the forest," said Peter. "You can see that she doesn't take very good care of your things. See how dirty it is? Some of the pages are torn, too. I wouldn't lend anything to someone who treats my stuff that way."

"I wouldn't either," Bob said, shaking his head. "This is a real shame. Here you go, Maggie."

Maggie took the journal from Bob and turned it over to look at the damage.

"Why did you give it to her?" asked Peter.

"Because it belongs to her." Bob pointed at the writing on the cover. "If you or your mother could read, you'd know that's Maggie's name. She wouldn't do this to her journal or to mine, which means that you did it. I don't take kindly to thieves or liars. Maybe I should contact the sheriff."

"I'm not a thief!" exclaimed Peter.

"Really?" said Bob. "You used your little sister to lure Maggie into the forest. While Maggie was trying to help a child who needed her, you stole the journal, thinking it belonged to me. I don't know which is worst: using your little sister like that, stealing the journal, lying about it, or trying to blame

Maggie for the damage you did to the book."

"Hey, at least I brought it back," Peter said grudgingly.

"Don't ever touch my stuff again, Peter!" Maggie told him.

Peter scowled and walked away.

Leonard kicked the side of his stall. "If he does, I'll tell the sheriff myself," he shouted, loud enough for Peter to hear. "And don't you ever say anything bad about Randal again. That unicorn is better with three legs than you are with two!"

Chapter 7

It was chilly out the next morning. Maggie had a hard time getting out of her warm, cozy bed, and Bob reached the stable before she did. He was scooping feed for Carmelita and her piglets when Maggie saw his hat. She couldn't help it; she giggled and then laughed out loud. When Bob turned to look at her, she covered her mouth with her hand and shook her head.

"That is the funniest hat I've ever seen!" she told him. The hat was long and pointed with a tassel on the end. Earflaps covered his ears, and another flap dangled in front of his forehead to cover his nose.

Bob shrugged. "Maybe, but it's the warmest hat I own. The only place I wear it is the stable. The horses don't seem to mind it. Even Leonard hasn't complained."

"That's because they don't know what hats usually look like," said Maggie. "What does Nora think of it?"

Bob grinned. "She thinks it's as funny as you do. Why do you think I don't wear it anyplace but here?"

"If it makes you happy . . ."

Maggie said, giggling as she walked off carrying the feed for the flying pigs.

After she'd fed the pigs and helped with the other animals, Maggie took Leonard for another ride. They decided on a change of scenery, so they rode around the castle, then down the road as far as the mill. The sun was shining, the day had warmed up, and Leonard was in a good mood.

"I'm tired of this pokey pace," he announced when they reached a straight stretch of road. "Hold on tight!"

Maggie barely had time to tighten her grip on the reins before they were off, racing through the forest. She was enjoying the wind on her face and the way her hair whipped behind her when suddenly there was a loud *crack!* as if a big branch had broken. A moment later, a huge animal ran out of the woods in a blur of fur and teeth. Leonard planted his front feet and slid to a stop. Maggie shrieked as she struggled to stay on the horse's back. The animal was gone by the time she was upright again.

"Sorry about that!" said Leonard. "Did you see that beast

run past? I thought we were going to run right into each other."

"I'm glad you were able to stop like that," Maggie told him.

"I think we should head home now," said Leonard. "I don't want to run into whatever that was again."

"Is that its paw print?" Maggie asked, pointing to a mark in the soft dirt at the edge of the road.

"Could be," said Leonard. "I wasn't exactly looking at its paws."

They had just turned around to head back to the stable when Maggie saw someone slipping between the trees. She thought it might be Peter, but she couldn't be sure.

Leonard trotted all the way back to the stable. After taking care of Leonard, Maggie put him in his stall and went to find Bob. She found him returning from a trip to the castle.

"How was your ride?" he asked.

"Great, until we almost ran into a huge beast, and I mean actually ran into it. The whole thing happened so fast that I didn't get a good look at it, but I think this was its paw print." Taking out her journal, Maggie drew the print as best she could.

"That looks like a manticore print," said Bob. "Running into a manticore like that could have been very bad, with terrible results."

"There was a loud sound in the forest right before the manticore came charging out. Later I thought I saw Peter in the woods," Maggie told him.

Bob sighed. "I wouldn't put it past Peter to startle a manticore just so it would run into Leonard. But then, there are a lot of things that I think Peter is capable of doing. I'm sure we haven't seen the last of him."

Chapter 8

The next day, Bob let Carmelita out of the barn for some fresh air and exercise. Maggie held the blanket while Bob tossed the piglets, but only one had a hard time flying. While the mother pig was still outside, Maggie cleaned the stall and played with the piglets. She was putting the pitchfork back where it belonged when she noticed the brush they had used for the palomino unicorn during its short stay in the stable. With the brush in her hand, she went to look for Bob.

"Would it be all right if I gave this brush to Lily?" Maggie called. "The palomino unicorn has been staying near her waterfall and they've gotten to be friends. When he was here, he loved it when she brushed him with this."

Bob stepped out of a stall to take a look. "Sure, give the brush to Lily. It will make both of them happy."

Maggie giggled. Bob was wearing his funny hat again and she laughed every time she saw it. He put on a pretend-serious face and said, "I'll have you know that this hat is very special to me! My dear old mother made me this hat when I was a young man. I love this hat, despite what other people might think."

"Your mother did a lovely job," Maggie said, trying to look just as serious.

"If you're going to the waterfall, can I go, too?" Leonard asked from the next stall. "I really like the taste of that water."

"Sure," said Maggie. "But please be nice to Lily. Water nymphs are sensitive people."

"People say rude stuff to me all the time!" Leonard replied with a snort. "Do you know how many people are shocked when I talk?"

"Even so . . ." Maggie began.

"All right! I'll be nice to your friend. But she had better be nice to me," Leonard finished under his breath.

When all her chores were done, Maggie saddled Leonard and led him out of the stable. As soon as she was on his back, the horse walked a short way before breaking into a trot. He slowed again as he entered the forest, and they heard shouting just ahead.

"I throw rocks best!" shouted a

goblin. "You watch. I hit turtle first try!"

"I better than you! I hit turtle now!" cried another.

"I recognize those voices," Leonard told Maggie.

"So do I!" Maggie replied.

Maggie was about to reach for the tip of a unicorn horn that she kept in her pocket when she saw Lily. The water nymph was walking out of the water toward the goblins with her own unicorn horn tip in her hand.

When the goblins saw the shining piece of horn, they screeched and ran into the forest.

"I'm happy to see you using it!" Maggie called to Lily.

The water nymph turned and smiled when she saw Maggie. "That little bit of unicorn horn has helped a lot!" Lily told her. "I love how it scares the goblins away. I still can't thank you enough for giving it to me."

"You deserved it after you helped

cure the unicorn," said Maggie. "Here, I brought you something."

Sliding off Leonard's back, she walked to the pool and handed the brush to Lily. "You said that the palomino unicorn was living around here. I know how much you both liked it when you brushed

him. Bob said that you could have this."

"That's so thoughtful!" said Lily. "Thank you! And please thank Bob for me too."

"I'm glad you like it," Maggie said, beaming. "I like giving things to people who appreciate them. My stepsiblings always took things without ever saying thank you. Peter was the worst."

"I saw him about an hour ago," said Lily. "He was heading toward the stable. Did he come to talk to you?"

Maggie shook her head. "I didn't see him."

"He was carrying a sack and had a big smile on his face," said Lily. "I had a feeling he was up to no good. I really don't like that boy."

Leonard snorted. "You're not the only one!"

Chapter 9

"I wonder what Peter was up to," Maggie said on the way back to the stable.

"Nothing good, I'm sure," said Leonard. "We'll look around when we get home."

Maggie worried the entire way.

As soon as they reached the stable, she slid off Leonard's back and began studying everything, trying to see if anything looked different. Lily had said that Peter was carrying a bag. Maybe he was planning to haul something away. Or maybe he had brought something that shouldn't be there. Everything looked the same, however, so she led Leonard into the barn to remove his saddle and bridle.

After putting Leonard back in

his stall, Maggie hurried to check on the piglets. There were a lot of rare and valuable animals in the stable, but the piglets and the tiny flying horses would be the easiest to steal. She counted the piglets and the tiny horses before looking in on the other animals. They were all

where they belonged, and they all seemed fine.

"Maybe Peter didn't come here after all," Maggie said as she looked in on Leonard one last time.

"Don't jump to any conclusions," replied the horse. "He might have gone to talk to Bob."

"That's true," said Maggie. She hoped Peter hadn't gone to pester Bob; none of the conversations Bob had had with either Peter or Zelia had ever gone very well. She didn't want Bob or Nora upset, especially not because of her.

Bob was writing a letter when Maggie walked into the cottage, but he set it aside when she stood in front of him.

"I took the brush to Lily," Maggie told him. "She asked me to thank you."

"I'm glad she liked it," Bob said. "You did a very nice thing, Maggie."

"Did Peter stop by while I was gone?" asked Maggie.

"If he did, I didn't see him," said Bob. "Why do you ask?"

"Lily said that she saw Peter headed this way with a bag. She thinks he might have been up to something."

THUD! THUD! came a sound from outside.

Startled, Maggie looked around as Bob got to his feet.

"What was that?" Maggie asked him.

"It sounds as if one of the

animals is cast in its stall," Bob said as he started to the door.

Maggie hurried after him. "What does that mean?"

"That an animal lay down in a stall too close to the wall and isn't able to get up," said Bob. "It's kicking the wall as it tries to stand. If it stays cast, it might hurt itself, so I have to help it get to its feet."

"Peter couldn't have caused this, could he?" Maggie asked.

"It's not likely," said Bob. They could still hear the thudding as they reached the stable. The sound led them straight to Leonard's stall. Maggie was relieved to see that he was standing and seemed to be fine.

"Why were you kicking your wall?" Bob asked him.

"It was a good way to get your attention," said Leonard. "Someone put nasty weeds in my hay. I'm positive they weren't here before we left. If I eat these, I'll get really sick."

Bob bent down to examine the

hay. "Leonard is right! Eating these weeds would make any animal sick. We'll have to throw out all this hay."

"I'll check the rest of the stalls and see if the weeds are in the other animals' hay," said Maggie.

"We need to check the hay in the loft, too," said Bob.

"Peter did this, didn't he?" Maggie asked.

Bob sighed. "You're probably right. I never have believed in coincidences."

Chapter 10

To Maggie's relief, the only place they found the bad weeds was in Leonard's hay. She had checked all the hay, including the bales in the loft, when Nora called her in for lunch. Bob had already eaten and was about to go out again just as Maggie walked in.

"Has anyone seen my hat?" asked Bob. "I know I put it on the hook by the door."

"If you're talking about that awful hat with the nose flap, I hope you lost it for good," said Nora. "I've never liked that thing and I've been tempted to throw it out more than once."

"I like it because it's warm," said Bob. "I'm going to look in the bedroom. Maybe I took it in there."

"I'll be right back," Maggie told Nora. "I got some hay under my tunic and it itches like crazy!"

Maggie hurried to her room to get cleaned up. Bob and Nora had given her some of their daughter's old clothes, which meant that she had two other tunics she could wear. Looking through her clothes, she found Bob's funny hat on the bottom of the pile.

"I found this buried under my clothes," Maggie said as she carried it to the kitchen. "I don't know why it would be there."

"That's odd," Bob said, frowning. "I know I didn't take it to your room."

"That is odd," said Nora. "And it reminds me about something odd that happened to me today, too. I went to collect eggs from the chickens this morning, like I do every day. When I came back in, the cottage door was open. I know I closed it because I remember jiggling the latch to get it to stay shut. It could have blown open if it was windy out, but there hasn't even been a breeze today."

"I asked the blacksmith to make a new latch," said Bob. "I need to visit him again to see if it's ready. You know, the three of us are the only ones who know about the problems we're having with the latch. Anyone else might think they'd shut the door and it would stay shut. It's possible that someone came inside while we were all out."

"And put your hat in Maggie's room?" said Nora. "Why would anyone do that?"

"Bob was telling me how much he loves that hat just this morning," said Maggie. "He said that his mother made it for him and it's very special."

"That old thing!" said Nora.

Bob frowned. "If someone heard me talking to Maggie, they might think I really did treasure it."

"And putting the hat in my room might make you think I had taken it," said Maggie.

"I suppose that's possible," Bob said, "but it would be a lousy thing to do. It sounds like something Peter might try."

Nora looked worried. "Maybe

we should get a dog that will bark when someone comes to the door."

"Or a big dog that will bite intruders. I want to keep everyone safe," Bob said, looking from Nora to Maggie.

"And maybe a good lock?" asked Nora.

"Sure," said Bob. "And a *really* big dog. I'll look around. I'm sure I can find something that would keep intruders out."

Chapter 11

When Stella stopped by the next morning, she helped Bob and Maggie give the piglets another flying lesson. After they fed raspberries to the tiny horses, Maggie went with Stella to get Eglantine out of the stall where the goose had been happily pecking at grain.

"Be careful when you go home," Maggie told her friend. "Peter has been coming around here a lot lately. I don't want him to try to steal Eglantine."

"I thought about that," said Stella. "That's why we came here in disguise. Here, Eglantine. Hop in."

When Stella set a basket on the floor of the stall, the goose hopped in and settled down. Stella picked up the basket and strapped it to her back, then tossed a faded gray cape over her shoulders. With the hood pulled low over her face, she looked like a frail old woman. The disguise was nearly perfect until Maggie got close enough to see Eglantine peeking over Stella's shoulder.

"That's great as long as you don't let Peter get close," Maggie said.

"I'm not going anywhere near Peter!" declared Stella. "I don't like that boy!"

"Neither do I!" said Maggie. She watched as her friend walked away, trying to move like an old woman. It was convincing enough if you didn't look too hard.

Bob was already bringing Leonard out of his stall when Maggie walked back inside. She held the horse's head while Bob trimmed his hooves. Then she took Leonard back into his stall and shut the door. Maggie was about to fetch Randal to get his hooves done when she heard Zelia's voice. Her stepmother was standing just inside the stable door talking to Bob. Peter was there, too, trying to hold onto a squirming sack.

"I came to tell you that you're making a big mistake," Zelia told Bob as Maggie walked up. "Maggie shouldn't be working here. She makes up stories and can't be trusted to do what you tell her. I don't know how many times she walked out on Peter when he needed her. She steals things, too. One day she took my red shawl and tried to make up a ridiculous story when I caught her. I'm sure you've found that things have gone missing in your home now that she's moved in."

Maggie felt her face turn red as

she listened to Zelia. These were the same things that her stepmother had accused her of doing all along, and none of it was true. Hearing it all again made Maggie mad. And she was sure that Peter had done such awful things over the last few days just to turn Bob against her. She didn't think Bob would believe Zelia, but what if he did? Could her stepmother ruin everything even now?

"If you ask me—" Leonard began.

"Not now, Leonard!" said Bob.

"If you need help, you should hire Peter," Zelia continued. "He's strong and smart and very reliable. He's good at finding magical animals, too. Show him what you found this morning, Peter."

"It's a flying pig," Peter said as he dumped the contents of the sack onto the floor.

Maggie gasped when she saw the little animal. It was a baby wild boar and wasn't much bigger than the piglets they'd been teaching to fly. Although it had wings, Maggie could tell right away that they weren't real. Someone had glued feathers onto the creature's sides. The little boar looked miserable. It was already biting at itself and squealing

as it tried to rip off the pretend wings.

"You see!" crowed Zelia. "My son can do a lot of things. I'm sure Maggie can't catch a flying pig."

"Watch out!" Peter shouted as the baby boar twisted in his hands and got away.

Maggie ran to shut the stable doors while her stepbrother lunged after the little pig. She and Bob watched as Peter chased the animal up and down the aisle.

Zelia tried to corner it, but the baby boar was too fast for her.

"I think I should help them," Maggie finally told Bob. "Otherwise they'll be at this all day and we won't get any more work done."

When Bob nodded, Maggie studied the little boar. The moment she saw the little animal coming toward her, she snatched it off the floor. Peter's jaw dropped when she dumped the boar into his hands.

"Actually," said Bob, "Maggie is

very good at catching flying piglets. She's had a lot of practice with the real ones. Now, I want you to take your little boar and leave. Trying to deceive me like that is not going to make me want to hire your son. I don't like liars!"

"We're not liars!" Zelia snapped.

"Nothing you said about Maggie is true, and that pig is not a real flying pig," said Bob. "You lied to me, and if you don't agree, we'll ask the sheriff what he thinks."

Zelia sneered at Bob. With her head held high, she turned and started to stalk from the stable. Maggie hurried to stand in her way.

"I thought you didn't believe in flying pigs," said Maggie. "When I told you about them, you said I'd made them up. What changed your mind?"

"Nothing changed my mind. I still don't believe they're real. But if pretending we do will get Peter a job, we'll say we believe anything," Zelia told her.

"And what about you?" Maggie said, turning to Peter. "Why do you want to work here?"

Peter shrugged. "We need the money. Mother says that if you can do it, so can I."

"Yes, but do you really want to work *here*?"

Peter snorted. "Not with that crazy old coot! Anyone who believes that flying pigs are real has got to be out of his mind."

"Is that so?" said Maggie. "Stay here. I'll be right back."

Carmelita was still outside taking a break from her babies, so it was safe for Maggie to go into the stall. Grabbing the closest piglet, Maggie carried it out of the stall and latched the door behind her.

"Hey, Zelia, catch!" Maggie called and tossed the piglet at her stepmother.

Zelia shrieked and threw up her hands as if to ward off the little pig. She gasped when the piglet began to fly. She made a squeaking sound when Bob caught it in midair.

"Now who's crazy?" Maggie asked, glancing from Zelia to Peter.

Zelia's jaw had dropped, but she closed it with a snap when she looked at Maggie. "You can keep your flying pigs and your crazy old man. We'll find other ways to make money. Come along, Peter."

Maggie watched as Peter hurried after his mother. When they were gone, she turned to Bob. "Thank you for believing in me. I don't know what I would have done if you had believed Zelia."

"I've never believed a word that woman has said," Bob replied. "There's no reason I should start now. If you ask me, your step-mother is crazy. Imagine thinking I would ever hire her son after all the things he's done! You, however, are one of the nicest, sweetest, most reliable girls I've ever met. You've never given me any reason to doubt you, and I don't think you ever will."

Maggie felt all warm inside when she heard what Bob said. She already felt as if he was the grandfather she'd never known. With a soft cry, she threw her arms around him. She was still giving him a hug when Nora came into the barn.

"Is everything all right?" she asked. "I saw that terrible woman walk out just now with her horrid

son. I hope they didn't say any-thing to upset our Maggie!"

"They didn't upset me," Maggie said and drew Nora into the hug. "And as long as I have you two, nothing they say will ever bother me again!"

"You've got me, too!" Leonard called from his stall. "Next time they come around, let me do the talking! I really want to give them a piece of my mind."

Maggie grinned. Who cared

about Zelia and Peter anyway? She had a family who really loved her, and in the end, that was all that mattered.

About the Author

E. D. Baker is the author of the Tales of the Frog Princess series, the Wide-Awake Princess series, the Fairy-Tale Matchmaker series, and many other delightful books for young readers, including *A Question of Magic*,

Fairy Wings, and *Fairy Lies*. Her first book, *The Frog Princess*, was the inspiration for Disney's hit movie *The Princess and the Frog*. She lives with her family and their many animals in rural Maryland.

www.talesofedbaker.com